Alfred Lord Tennyson

The Last Tournament

Outlook

Alfred Lord Tennyson

The Last Tournament

1. Auflage | ISBN: 978-3-73262-766-0

Erscheinungsort: Frankfurt am Main, Deutschland

Erscheinungsjahr: 2018

Outlook Verlag GmbH, Frankfurt.

THE LAST TOURNAMENT

BY

ALFRED TENNYSON, D.C.L.,

POET-LAUREATE

AUTHOR'S EDITION

FROM ADVANCE SHEETS

This poem forms one of the "Idyls of the King." Its place is between "Pelleas" and "Guinevere."

BY ALFRED TENNYSON,

POET LAUREATE

   Dagonet, the fool, whom Gawain in his moods
Had made mock-knight of Arthur's Table Round,
At Camelot, high above the yellowing woods,
Danced like a wither'd leaf before the Hall.
And toward him from the Hall, with harp in hand,
And from the crown thereof a carcanet
Of ruby swaying to and fro, the prize
Of Tristram in the jousts of yesterday,
Came Tristram, saying, "Why skip ye so, Sir Fool?"

   For Arthur and Sir Lancelot riding once
Far down beneath a winding wall of rock
Heard a child wail. A stump of oak half-dead,
From roots like some black coil of carven snakes
Clutch'd at the crag, and started thro' mid-air
Bearing an eagle's nest: and thro' the tree
Rush'd ever a rainy wind, and thro' the wind
Pierced ever a child's cry: and crag and tree
Scaling, Sir Lancelot from the perilous nest,
This ruby necklace thrice around her neck,
And all unscarr'd from beak or talon, brought
A maiden babe; which Arthur pitying took,
Then gave it to his Queen to rear: the Queen
But coldly acquiescing, in her white arms
Received, and after loved it tenderly,
And named it Nestling; so forgot herself
A moment, and her cares; till that young life
Being smitten in mid-heaven with mortal cold
Past from her; and in time the carcanet
Vext her with plaintive memories of the child:
So she, delivering it to Arthur, said,
"Take thou the jewels of this dead innocence,

2

And make them, an thou wilt, a tourney-prize."

To whom the King, "Peace to thine eagle-borne
Dead nestling, and this honor after death,
Following thy will! but, O my Queen, I muse
Why ye not wear on arm, or neck, or zone, Those
diamonds that I rescued from the tarn, And
Lancelot won, methought, for thee to wear."

"Would rather ye had let them fall," she cried,
"Plunge and be lost—ill-fated as they were,
A bitterness to me!—ye look amazed,
Not knowing they were lost as soon as given—
Slid from my hands, when I was leaning out
Above the river—that unhappy child
Past in her barge: but rosier luck will go
With these rich jewels, seeing that they came
Not from the skeleton of a brother-slayer,
But the sweet body of a maiden babe.
Perchance—who knows?—the purest of thy knights
May win them for the purest of my maids."

She ended, and the cry of a great jousts
With trumpet-blowings ran on all the ways
From Camelot in among the faded fields
To furthest towers; and everywhere the knights
Arm'd for a day of glory before the King.

But on the hither side of that loud morn
Into the hall stagger'd, his visage ribb'd
From ear to ear with dogwhip-weals, his nose
Bridge-broken, one eye out, and one hand off,
And one with shatter'd fingers dangling lame,
A churl, to whom indignantly the King,
"My churl, for whom Christ died, what evil beast
Hath drawn his claws athwart thy face? or fiend?
Man was it who marr'd Heaven's image in thee thus?"

Then, sputtering thro' the hedge of splinter'd teeth,
Yet strangers to the tongue, and with blunt stump
Pitch-blacken'd sawing the air, said the maim'd churl,
"He took them and he drave them to his tower—
Some hold he was a table-knight of thine—
A hundred goodly ones—the Red Knight, he—

"Lord, I was tending swine, and the Red Knight
Brake in upon me and drave them to his tower;
And when I call'd upon thy name as one
That doest right by gentle and by churl,
Maim'd me and maul'd, and would outright have slain,
Save that he sware me to a message, saying—
'Tell thou the King and all his liars, that I
Have founded my Round Table in the North,
And whatsoever his own knights have sworn
My knights have sworn the counter to it—and say
My tower is full of harlots, like his court,
But mine are worthier, seeing they profess
To be none other than themselves—and say
My knights are all adulterers like his own,
But mine are truer, seeing they profess
To be none other; and say his hour is come,
The heathen are upon him, his long lance
Broken, and his Excalibur a straw.'"

Then Arthur turn'd to Kay the seneschal,
"Take thou my churl, and tend him curiously
Like a king's heir, till all his hurts be whole.
The heathen—but that ever-climbing wave,
Hurl'd back again so often in empty foam,
Hath lain for years at rest—and renegades,
Thieves, bandits, leavings of confusion, whom
The wholesome realm is purged of otherwhere,—
Friends, thro' your manhood and your fealty,—now
Make their last head like Satan in the North.
My younger knights, new-made, in whom your flower
Waits to be solid fruit of golden deeds,
Move with me toward their quelling, which achieved,
The loneliest ways are safe from shore to shore.
But thou, Sir Lancelot, sitting in my place
Enchair'd to-morrow, arbitrate the field;
For wherefore shouldst thou care to mingle with it,
Only to yield my Queen her own again?
Speak, Lancelot, thou art silent: is it well?"

* * * * *

Thereto Sir Lancelot answer'd, "It is well:
Yet better if the King abide, and leave

4

The leading of his younger knights to me.
Else, for the King has will'd it, it is well."

* * * * *

Then Arthur rose and Lancelot follow'd him,
And while they stood without the doors, the King
Turn'd to him saying, "Is it then so well?
Or mine the blame that oft I seem as he
Of whom was written, 'a sound is in his ears'—
The foot that loiters, bidden go,—the glance
That only seems half-loyal to command,—
A manner somewhat fall'n from reverence—
Or have I dream'd the bearing of our knights
Tells of a manhood ever less and lower?
Or whence the fear lest this my realm, uprear'd,
By noble deeds at one with noble vows,
From flat confusion and brute violences,
Reel back into the beast, and be no more?"

* * * * *

He spoke, and taking all his younger knights,
Down the slope city rode, and sharply turn'd
North by the gate. In her high bower the Queen,
Working a tapestry, lifted up her head,
Watch'd her lord pass, and knew not that she sigh'd.
Then ran across her memory the strange rhyme
Of bygone Merlin, "Where is he who knows?
From the great deep to the great deep he goes."

* * * * *

But when the morning of a tournament,
By these in earnest those in mockery call'd
The Tournament of the Dead Innocence,
Brake with a wet wind blowing, Lancelot,
Round whose sick head all night, like birds of prey,
The words of Arthur flying shriek'd, arose,
And down a streetway hung with folds of pure
White samite, and by fountains running wine,
Where children sat in white with cups of gold,
Moved to the lists, and there, with slow sad steps
Ascending, fill'd his double-dragon'd chair.

* * * * *

He glanced and saw the stately galleries,
Dame, damsel, each thro' worship of their Queen
White-robed in honor of the stainless child,
And some with scatter'd jewels, like a bank
Of maiden snow mingled with sparks of fire.
He lookt but once, and veil'd his eyes again.

* * * * *

   The sudden trumpet sounded as in a dream
To ears but half-awaked, then one low roll
Of Autumn thunder, and the jousts began:
And ever the wind blew, and yellowing leaf
And gloom and gleam, and shower and shorn plume
Went down it. Sighing weariedly, as one
Who sits and gazes on a faded fire,
When all the goodlier guests are past away,
Sat their great umpire, looking o'er the lists.
He saw the laws that ruled the tournament
Broken, but spake not; once, a knight cast down
Before his throne of arbitration cursed
The dead babe and the follies of the King;
And once the laces of a helmet crack'd,
And show'd him, like a vermin in its hole,
Modred, a narrow face: anon he heard
The voice that billow'd round the barriers roar
An ocean-sounding welcome to one knight,
But newly-enter'd, taller than the rest,
And armor'd all in forest green, whereon
There tript a hundred tiny silver deer,
And wearing but a holly-spray for crest,
With ever-scattering berries, and on shield
A spear, a harp, a bugle—Tristram—late
From overseas in Brittany return'd,
And marriage with a princess of that realm,
Isolt the White—Sir Tristram of the Woods—
Whom Lancelot knew, had held sometime with pain
His own against him, and now yearn'd to shake
The burthen off his heart in one full shock
With Tristram ev'n to death: his strong hands gript
And dinted the gilt dragons right and left,
Until he groan'd for wrath—so many of those,
That ware their ladies' colors on the casque,

Drew from before Sir Tristram to the bounds,
And there with gibes and nickering mockeries
Stood, while he mutter'd, "Craven chests! O shame!
What faith have these in whom they sware to love?
The glory of our Round Table is no more."

* * * * *

So Tristram won, and Lancelot gave, the gems,
Not speaking other word than "Hast thou won?
Art thou the purest, brother? See, the hand
Wherewith thou takest this is red!" to whom
Tristram, half plagued by Lancelot's languorous mood,
Made answer, "Ay, but wherefore toss me this
Like a dry bone cast to some hungry hound?
Let be thy fair Queen's fantasy. Strength of heart
And might of limb, but mainly use and skill,
Are winners in this pastime of our King.
My hand—belike the lance hath dript upon it—
No blood of mine, I trow; but O chief knight,
Right arm of Arthur in the battlefield,
Great brother, thou nor I have made the world;
Be happy in thy fair Queen as I in mine."
And Tristram round the gallery made his horse
Caracole; then bow'd his homage, bluntly saying,
"Fair damsels, each to him who worships each
Sole Queen of Beauty and of love, behold
This day my Queen of Beauty is not here."
Then most of these were mute, some anger'd, one
Murmuring "All courtesy is dead," and one,
"The glory of our Round Table is no more."

Then fell thick rain, plume droopt and mantle clung,
And pettish cries awoke, and the wan day
Went glooming down in wet and weariness:
But under her black brows a swarthy dame
Laught shrilly, crying "Praise the patient saints,
Our one white day of Innocence hath past,
Tho' somewhat draggled at the skirt. So be it.
The snowdrop only, flow'ring thro' the year,
Would make the world as blank as wintertide.
Come—let us comfort their sad eyes, our Queen's
And Lancelot's, at this night's solemnity

With all the kindlier colors of the field."

* * * * *

So dame and damsel glitter'd at the feast
Variously gay: for he that tells the tale
Liken'd them, saying "as when an hour of cold
Falls on the mountain in midsummer snows,
And all the purple slopes of mountain flowers
Pass under white, till the warm hour returns
With veer of wind, and all are flowers again;"
So dame and damsel cast the simple white,
And glowing in all colors, the live grass,
Rose-campion, bluebell, kingcup, poppy, glanced
About the revels, and with mirth so loud
Beyond all use, that, half-amazed, the Queen,
And wroth at Tristram and the lawless jousts,
Brake up their sports, then slowly to her bower
Parted, and in her bosom pain was lord.

* * * * *

And little Dagonet on the morrow morn,
High over all the yellowing Autumn-tide,
Danced like a wither'd leaf before the hall.
Then Tristram saying, "Why skip ye so, Sir Fool?"
Wheel'd round on either heel, Dagonet replied,
"Belike for lack of wiser company;
Or being fool, and seeing too much wit
Makes the world rotten, why, belike I skip
To know myself the wisest knight of all."
"Ay, fool," said Tristram, "but 'tis eating dry
To dance without a catch, a roundelay
To dance to." Then he twangled on his harp,
And while he twangled little Dagonet stood,
Quiet as any water-sodden log
Stay'd in the wandering warble of a brook;
But when the twangling ended, skip again;
Then being ask'd, "Why skipt ye not, Sir Fool?"
Made answer, "I had liefer twenty years
Skip to the broken music of my brains
Than any broken music ye can make."
Then Tristram, waiting for the quip to come,
"Good now, what music have I broken, fool?"

And little Dagonet, skipping, "Arthur, the king's;
For when thou playest that air with Queen Isolt,
Thou makest broken music with thy bride,
Her daintier namesake down in Brittany—
And so thou breakest Arthur's music too."
"Save for that broken music in thy brains,
Sir Fool," said Tristram, "I would break thy head.
Fool, I came late, the heathen wars were o'er,
The life had flown, we sware but by the shell—
I am but a fool to reason with a fool
Come, thou art crabb'd and sour: but lean me down,
Sir Dagonet, one of thy long asses' ears,
And hearken if my music be not true.

"'Free love—free field—we love but while we may:
The woods are hush'd, their music is no more:
The leaf is dead, the yearning past away:
New leaf, new life—the days of frost are o'er:
New life, new love to suit the newer day:
New loves are sweet as those that went before:
Free love,—free field—we love but while we may.'

"Ye might have moved slow-measure to my tune,
Not stood stockstill. I made it in the woods,
And found it ring as true as tested gold."

But Dagonet with one foot poised in his hand,
"Friend, did ye mark that fountain yesterday
Made to run wine?—but this had run itself
All out like a long life to a sour end—
And them that round it sat with golden cups
To hand the wine to whomsoever came—
The twelve small damosels white as Innocence,

"In honor of poor Innocence the babe,
Who left the gems which Innocence the Queen
Lent to the King, and Innocence the King
Gave for a prize—and one of those white slips
Handed her cup and piped, the pretty one,
'Drink, drink, Sir Fool,' and thereupon I drank,
Spat—pish—the cup was gold, the draught was mud."
And Tristram, "Was it muddier than thy gibes?
Is all the laughter gone dead out of thee?—
Not marking how the knighthood mock thee, fool—

'Fear God: honor the king—his one true knight—
Sole follower of the vows'—for here be they
Who knew thee swine enow before I came,
Smuttier than blasted grain: but when the King
Had made thee fool, thy vanity so shot up
It frighted all free fool from out thy heart;
Which left thee less than fool, and less than swine,
A naked aught—yet swine I hold thee still,
For I have flung thee pearls, and find thee swine."

　　And little Dagonet mincing with his feet,
"Knight, an ye fling those rubies round my neck
In lieu of hers, I'll hold thou hast some touch
Of music, since I care not for thy pearls.
Swine? I have wallow'd, I have wash'd—the world
Is flesh and shadow—I have had my day.
The dirty nurse, Experience, in her kind
Hath foul'd me—an I wallow'd, then I wash'd—
I have had my day and my philosophies—
And thank the Lord I am King Arthur's fool.
Swine, say ye? swine, goats, asses, rams and geese
Troop'd round a Paynim harper once, who thrumm'd
On such a wire as musically as thou
Some such fine song—but never a king's fool."

　　And Tristram, "Then were swine, goats, asses, geese
The wiser fools, seeing thy Paynim bard
Had such a mastery of his mystery
That he could harp his wife up out of Hell."

　　Then Dagonet, turning on the ball of his foot,
"And whither harp'st thou thine? down! and thyself
Down! and two more: a helpful harper thou,
That harpest downward! Dost thou know the star
We call the harp of Arthur up in heaven?"

　　And Tristram, "Ay, Sir Fool, for when our King
Was victor wellnigh day by day, the knights,
Glorying in each new glory, set his name
High on all hills, and in the signs of heaven."

　　And Dagonet answer'd, "Ay, and when the land
Was freed, and the Queen false, ye set yourself
To babble about him, all to show your wit—
And whether he were king by courtesy,

Or king by right—and so went harping down
The black king's highway, got so far, and grew
So witty, that ye play'd at ducks and drakes
With Arthur's vows on the great lake of fire.
Tuwhoo! do ye see it? do ye see the star?"
"Nay, fool," said Tristram, "not in open day."
And Dagonet, "Nay, nor will: I see it and hear.
It makes a silent music up in heaven,
And I, and Arthur and the angels hear,
And then we skip." "Lo, fool," he said, "ye talk
Fool's treason: is the king thy brother fool?"
Then little Dagonet clapt his hands and shrill'd,
"Ay, ay, my brother fool, the king of fools*!
Conceits himself as God that he can make
Figs out of thistles, silk from bristles, milk
From burning spurge, honey from hornet-combs,
And men from beasts.—Long live the king of fools!"

   And down the city Dagonet danced away.
But thro' the slowly-mellowing avenues
And solitary passes of the wood
Rode Tristram toward Lyonesse and the west.
Before him fled the face of Queen Isolt
With ruby-circled neck, but evermore
Past, as a rustle or twitter in the wood
Made dull his inner, keen his outer eye
For all that walk'd, or crept, or perched, or flew.
Anon the face, as, when a gust hath blown,
Unruffling waters re-collect the shape
Of one that in them sees himself, return'd;
But at the slot or fewmets of a deer,
Or ev'n a fall'n feather, vanish'd again.

   So on for all that day from lawn to lawn
Thro' many a league-long bower he rode. At length
A lodge of intertwisted beechen-boughs
Furze-cramm'd, and bracken-rooft, the which himself
Built for a summer day with Queen Isolt
Against a shower, dark in the golden grove
Appearing, sent his fancy back to where
She lived a moon in that low lodge with him:
Till Mark her lord had past, the Cornish king,
With six or seven, when Tristram was away,

And snatch'd her thence; yet dreading worse than shame
Her warrior Tristram, spake not any word,
But bode his hour, devising wretchedness.

   And now that desert lodge to Tristram lookt
So sweet, that, halting, in he past, and sank
Down on a drift of foliage random-blown;
But could not rest for musing how to smooth
And sleek his marriage over to the Queen.
Perchance in lone Tintagil far from all
The tonguesters of the court she had not heard.
But then what folly had sent him overseas
After she left him lonely here? a name?
Was it the name of one in Brittany,
Isolt, the daughter of the King? "Isolt
Of the white hands" they call'd her: the sweet name
Allured him first, and then the maid herself,
Who served him well with those white hands of hers,
And loved him well, until himself had thought
He loved her also, wedded easily,
But left her all as easily, and return'd.
The black-blue Irish hair and Irish eyes
Had drawn him home—what marvel? then he laid
His brows upon the drifted leaf and dream'd.

   He seem'd to pace the strand of Brittany
Between Isolt of Britain and his bride,
And show'd them both the ruby-chain, and both
Began to struggle for it, till his Queen
Graspt it so hard, that all her hand was red.
Then cried the Breton, "Look, her hand is red!
These be no rubies, this is frozen blood,
And melts within her hand—her hand is hot
With ill desires, but this I gave thee, look, Is
all as cool and white as any flower."
Follow'd a rush of eagle's wings, and then
A whimpering of the spirit of the child,
Because the twain had spoil'd her carcanet.

   He dream'd; but Arthur with a hundred spears
Rode far, till o'er the illimitable reed,
And many a glancing plash and sallowy isle,
The wide-wing'd sunset of the misty marsh

Glared on a huge machicolated tower
That stood with open doors, whereout was roll'd
A roar of riot, as from men secure
Amid their marshes, ruffians at their ease
Among their harlot-brides, an evil song.
"Lo there," said one of Arthur's youth, for there,
High on a grim dead tree before the tower,
A goodly brother of The Table Round
Swung by the neck: and on the boughs a shield
Showing a shower of blood in a field noir,
And therebeside a horn, inflamed the knights
At that dishonor done the gilded spur,
Till each would clash the shield, and blow the horn.
But Arthur waved them back: alone he rode.
Then at the dry harsh roar of the great horn,
That sent the face of all the marsh aloft

   An ever upward-rushing storm and cloud
Of shriek and plume, the Red Knight heard, and all,
Even to tipmost lance and topmost helm,
In blood-red armor sallying, howl'd to the King,
"The teeth of Hell flay bare and gnash thee flat!—
Lo! art thou not that eunuch-hearted King
Who fain had clipt free manhood from the world—
The woman-worshipper? Yea, God's curse, and I!
Slain was the brother of my paramour
By a knight of thine, and I that heard her whine
And snivel, being eunuch-hearted too,
Sware by the scorpion-worm that twists in hell,
And stings itself to everlasting death,
To hang whatever knight of thine I fought
And tumbled. Art thou King?—Look to thy life!"
He ended: Arthur knew the voice; the face
Wellnigh was helmet-hidden, and the name
Went wandering somewhere darkling in his mind.
And Arthur deign'd not use of word or sword,
But let the drunkard, as he stretch'd from horse
To strike him, overbalancing his bulk,
Down from the causeway heavily to the swamp
Fall, as the crest of some slow-arching wave
Heard in dead night along that table-shore
Drops flat, and after the great waters break

Whitening for half a league, and thin themselves
Far over sands marbled with moon and cloud.
From less and less to nothing; thus he fell
Head-heavy, while the knights, who watch'd him, roar'd
And shouted and leapt down upon the fall'n;
There trampled out his face from being known,
And sank his head in mire, and slimed themselves:
Nor heard the King for their own cries, but sprang
Thro' open doors, and swording right and left
Men, women, on their sodden faces, hurl'd
The tables over and the wines, and slew
Till all the rafters rang with woman-yells,
And all the pavement stream'd with massacre:
Then, yell with yell echoing, they fired the tower,
Which half that autumn night, like the live North,
Red-pulsing up thro' Alioth and Alcor,
Made all above it, and a hundred meres
About it, as the water Moab saw
Come round by the East, and out beyond them flush'd
The long low dune, and lazy-plunging sea.

   So all the ways were safe from shore to shore,
But in the heart of Arthur pain was lord.
Then out of Tristram waking the red dream
Fled with a shout, and that low lodge return'd,
Mid-forest, and the wind among the boughs.
He whistled his good warhorse left to graze
Among the forest greens, vaulted upon him,
And rode beneath an ever-showering leaf,
Till one lone woman, weeping near a cross,
Stay'd him, "Why weep ye?" "Lord," she said, "my man
Hath left me or is dead;" whereon he thought—
"What an she hate me now? I would not this.
What an she love me still? I would not that.
I know not what I would"—but said to her,—
"Yet weep not thou, lest, if thy mate return,
He find thy favor changed and love thee not"—
Then pressing day by day thro' Lyonesse
Last in a roky hollow, belling, heard
The hounds of Mark, and felt the goodly hounds
Yelp at his heart, but, turning, past and gain'd
Tintagil, half in sea, and high on land,

A crown of towers.

Down in a casement sat,
A low sea-sunset glorying round her hair
And glossy-throated grace, Isolt the Queen.
And when she heard the feet of Tristram grind
The spiring stone that scaled about her tower,
Flush'd, started, met him at the doors, and there
Belted his body with her white embrace,
Crying aloud, "Not Mark—not Mark, my soul!
The footstep flutter'd me at first: not he:
Catlike thro' his own castle steals my Mark,
But warrior-wise thou stridest through his halls
Who hates thee, as I him—ev'n to the death.
My soul, I felt my hatred for my Mark
Quicken within me, and knew that thou wert nigh."
To whom Sir Tristram smiling, "I am here.
Let be thy Mark, seeing he is not thine."

And drawing somewhat backward she replied,
"Can he be wrong'd who is not ev'n his own,
But save for dread of thee had beaten me,
Scratch'd, bitten, blinded, marr'd me somehow—Mark?
What rights are his that dare not strike for them?
Not lift a hand—not, tho' he found me thus!
But hearken, have ye met him? hence he went
To-day for three days' hunting—as he said—
And so returns belike within an hour.
Mark's way, my soul!—but eat not thou with him,
Because he hates thee even more than fears;
Nor drink: and when thou passest any wood
Close visor, lest an arrow from the bush
Should leave me all alone with Mark and hell.
My God, the measure of my hate for Mark
Is as the measure of my love for thee."

So, pluck'd one way by hate and one by love,
Drain'd of her force, again she sat, and spake
To Tristram, as he knelt before her, saying,
"O hunter, and O blower of the horn,
Harper, and thou hast been a rover too,
For, ere I mated with my shambling king,
Ye twain had fallen out about the bride

Of one—his name is out of me—the prize,
If prize she were—(what marvel—she could see)—
Thine, friend; and ever since my craven seeks
To wreck thee villanously: but, O Sir Knight,
What dame or damsel have ye kneeled to last?"

And Tristram, "Last to my Queen Paramount,
Here now to my Queen Paramount of love,
And loveliness, ay, lovelier than when first
Her light feet fell on our rough Lyonesse,
Sailing from Ireland."

Softly laugh'd Isolt,
"Flatter me not, for hath not our great Queen
My dole of beauty trebled?" and he said,
"Her beauty is her beauty, and thine thine,
And thine is more to me—soft, gracious, kind—
Save when thy Mark is kindled on thy lips
Most gracious; but she, haughty, ev'n to him,
Lancelot; for I have seen him wan enow
To make one doubt if ever the great Queen
Have yielded him her love."

To whom Isolt,
"Ah then, false hunter and false harper, thou
Who brakest thro' the scruple of my bond,
Calling me thy white hind, and saying to me
That Guinevere had sinned against the highest,
And I—misyoked with such a want of man—
That I could hardly sin against the lowest."

He answer'd, "O my soul, be comforted!
If this be sweet, to sin in leading-strings,
If here be comfort, and if ours be sin,
Crown'd warrant had we for the crowning sin
That made us happy: but how ye greet me—fear
And fault and doubt—no word of that fond tale—
Thy deep heart-yearnings, thy sweet memories
Of Tristram in that year he was away."

And, saddening on the sudden, spake Isolt,
"I had forgotten all in my strong joy
To see thee—yearnings?—ay! for, hour by hour,
Here in the never-ended afternoon,
O sweeter than all memories of thee,

Deeper than any yearnings after thee
Seem'd those far-rolling, westward-smiling seas,
Watched from this tower. Isolt of Britain dash'd
Before Isolt of Brittany on the strand,
Would that have chill'd her bride-kiss? Wedded her?
Fought in her father's battles? wounded there?
The King was all fulfill'd with gratefulness,
And she, my namesake of the hands, that heal'd
Thy hurt and heart with unguent and caress—
Well—can I wish her any huger wrong
Than having known thee? her too hast thou left
To pine and waste in those sweet memories?
O were I not my Mark's, by whom all men
Are noble, I should hate thee more than love."

    And Tristram, fondling her light hands, replied,
"Grace, Queen, for being loved: she loved me well.
Did I love her? the name at least I loved.
Isolt?—I fought his battles, for Isolt!
The night was dark; the true star set. Isolt!
The name was ruler of the dark——Isolt?
Care not for her! patient, and prayerful, meek,
Pale-blooded, she will yield herself to God."
And Isolt answer'd, "Yea, and why not I?
Mine is the larger need, who am not meek,
Pale-blooded, prayerful. Let me tell thee now.
Here one black, mute midsummer night I sat
Lonely, but musing on thee, wondering where,
Murmuring a light song I had heard thee sing,
And once or twice I spake thy name aloud.
Then flash'd a levin-brand; and near me stood,
In fuming sulphur blue and green, a fiend—
Mark's way to steal behind one in the dark—
For there was Mark: 'He has wedded her,' he said,
Not said, but hiss'd it: then this crown of towers
So shook to such a roar of all the sky,
That here in utter dark I swoon'd away,
And woke again in utter dark, and cried,
'I will flee hence and give myself to God'—
And thou wert lying in thy new leman's arms."

    Then Tristram, ever dallying with her hand,
"May God be with thee, sweet, when old and gray,

And past desire!" a saying that anger'd her.
"'May God be with thee, sweet, when thou art old,
And sweet no more to me!' I need Him now.
For when had Lancelot utter'd aught so gross
Ev'n to the swineherd's malkin in the mast?
The greater man, the greater courtesy.
But thou, thro' ever harrying thy wild beasts—
Save that to touch a harp, tilt with a lance
Becomes thee well—art grown wild beast thyself.
How darest thou, if lover, push me even
In fancy from thy side, and set me far
In the gray distance, half a life away,
Her to be loved no more? Unsay it, unswear!
Flatter me rather, seeing me so weak,
Broken with Mark and hate and solitude,
Thy marriage and mine own, that I should suck
Lies like sweet wines: lie to me: I believe.
Will ye not lie? not swear, as there ye kneel,
And solemnly as when ye sware to him,
The man of men, our King—My God, the power
Was once in vows when men believed the King!
They lied not then, who sware, and thro' their vows
The King prevailing made his realm:—I say,
Swear to me thou wilt love me ev'n when old,
Gray-haired, and past desire, and in despair."

  Then Tristram, pacing moodily up and down,
"Vows! did ye keep the vow ye made to Mark
More than I mine? Lied, say ye? Nay, but learnt,
The vow that binds too strictly snaps itself—
My knighthood taught me this—ay, being snapt—
We run more counter to the soul thereof
Than had we never sworn. I swear no more.
I swore to the great King, and am forsworn.
For once—ev'n to the height—I honor'd him.
'Man, is he man at all?' methought, when first
I rode from our rough Lyonesse, and beheld
That victor of the Pagan throned in hall—
His hair, a sun that ray'd from off a brow
Like hillsnow high in heaven, the steel-blue eyes,
The golden beard that clothed his lips with light—
Moreover, that weird legend of his birth,

With Merlin's mystic babble about his end,
Amazed me; then, his foot was on a stool
Shaped as a dragon; he seem'd to me no man,
But Michael trampling Satan; so I sware,
Being amazed: but this went by—the vows!
O ay—the wholesome madness of an hour—
They served their use, their time; for every knight
Believed himself a greater than himself,
And every follower eyed him as a God;
Till he, being lifted up beyond himself,
Did mightier deeds than elsewise he had done,
And so the realm was made; but then their vows—
First mainly thro' that sullying of our Queen—
Began to gall the knighthood, asking whence
Had Arthur right to bind them to himself?
Dropt down from heaven? wash'd up from out the deep?
They fail'd to trace him thro' the flesh and blood
Of our old Kings: whence then? a doubtful lord
To bind them by inviolable vows,
Which flesh and blood perforce would violate:
For feel this arm of mine—the tide within
Red with free chase and heather-scented air,
Pulsing full man; can Arthur make me pure
As any maiden child? lock up my tongue
From uttering freely what I freely hear?
Bind me to one? The great world laughs at it.
And worldling of the world am I, and know
The ptarmigan that whitens ere his hour
Wooes his own end; we are not angels here
Nor shall be: vows—I am woodman of the woods,
And hear the garnet-headed yaffingale
Mock them: my soul, we love but while we may;
And therefore is my love so large for thee,
Seeing it is not bounded save by love."

Here ending, he moved toward her, and she said,
"Good: an I turn'd away my love for thee
To some one thrice as courteous as thyself—
For courtesy wins woman all as well
As valor may—but he that closes both
Is perfect, he is Lancelot—taller indeed,
Rosier, and comelier, thou—but say I loved

This knightliest of all knights, and cast thee back
Thine own small saw 'We love but while we may,'
Well then, what answer?"

    He that while she spake,
Mindful of what he brought to adorn her with,
The jewels, had let one finger lightly touch
The warm white apple of her throat, replied,
"Press this a little closer, sweet, until—
Come, I am hunger'd and half-anger'd—meat,
Wine, wine—and I will love thee to the death,
And out beyond into the dream to come."

    So then, when both were brought to full accord,
She rose, and set before him all he will'd;
And after these had comforted the blood
With meats and wines, and satiated their hearts—
Now talking of their woodland paradise,
The deer, the dews, the fern, the founts, the lawns;
Now mocking at the much ungainliness,
And craven shifts, and long crane legs of Mark—
Then Tristram laughing caught the harp, and sang:

    "Ay, ay, O ay—the winds that bend the brier!
A star in heaven, a star within the mere!
Ay, ay, O ay—a star was my desire,
And one was far apart, and one was near:
Ay, ay, O ay—the winds that bow the grass!
And one was water and one star was fire,
And one will ever shine and one will pass.
Ay, ay, O ay—the winds that move the mere."

    Then in the light's last glimmer Tristram show'd
And swung the ruby carcanet. She cried,
"The collar of some order, which our King
Hath newly founded, all for thee, my soul,
For thee, to yield thee grace beyond thy peers."
"Not so, my Queen," he said, "but the red fruit
Grown on a magic oak-tree in mid-heaven,
And won by Tristram as a tourney-prize,
And hither brought by Tristram for his last
Love-offering and peace-offering unto thee."

    He rose, he turn'd, and flinging round her neck,
Claspt it; but while he bow'd himself to lay

Warm kisses in the hollow of her throat,
Out of the dark, just as the lips had touch'd,
Behind him rose a shadow and a shriek—
"Mark's way," said Mark, and clove him thro' the brain.

  That night came Arthur home, and while he climb'd,
All in a death-dumb autumn-dripping gloom,
The stairway to the hall, and look'd and saw
The great Queen's bower was dark,—about his feet
A voice clung sobbing till he question'd it,
"What art thou?" and the voice about his feet
Sent up an answer, sobbing, "I am thy fool,
And I shall never make thee smile again."

www.ingramcontent.com/pod-product-compliance
Lightning Source LLC
Chambersburg PA
CBHW022008050726
47499CB00009BA/3206